JAMES

PERCY

First published in Great Britain 1991
by Buzz Books, an imprint of Reed Children's Books
Michelin House, 81 Fulham Road, London SW3 6RB
and Auckland, Melbourne, Singapore and Toronto

Reprinted 1993

Copyright © William Heinemann Limited 1991

All publishing rights: William Heinemann Limited.
All television and merchandising rights licensed by
William Heinemann Limited to Britt Allcroft (Thomas) Limited
exclusively, worldwide.

Photographs © Britt Allcroft (Thomas) Limited 1985, 1986
Photographs by David Mitton and Terry Permane
for Britt Allcroft's production of Thomas the Tank
Engine and Friends

ISBN 1 85591 119 1

Printed in Italy by LEGO

THOMAS, PERCY AND THE COAL

buzz books

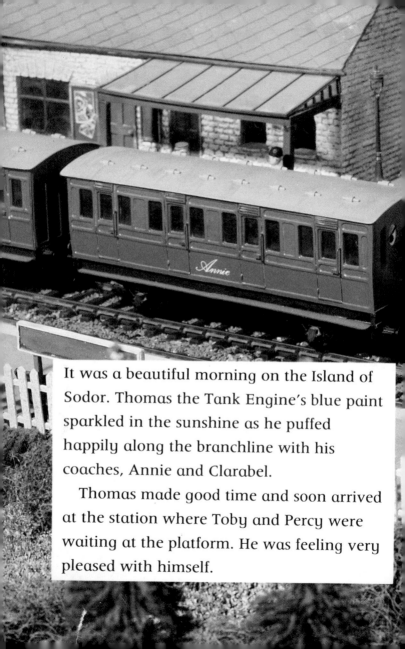

It was a beautiful morning on the Island of Sodor. Thomas the Tank Engine's blue paint sparkled in the sunshine as he puffed happily along the branchline with his coaches, Annie and Clarabel.

Thomas made good time and soon arrived at the station where Toby and Percy were waiting at the platform. He was feeling very pleased with himself.

"Hello, Thomas!" whistled Percy. "You look splendid!"

"Yes, indeed," boasted Thomas. "Blue is the only proper colour for an engine."

"Oh, I don't know. I like my brown paint," said Toby.

"I've always been green. I wouldn't want to be any other colour either," added Percy.

"Well, anyway," huffed Thomas, "blue is the only colour for a Really Useful Engine – everyone knows that."

Percy said no more; he just grinned at Toby. They knew only too well that sometimes Thomas could be a little too cheeky for his own good.

Later, Thomas was resting in a siding when Percy arrived in the yard. Percy pulled his trucks to a large hopper to load them with coal.

Thomas was still being cheeky.

"Careful, Percy," he warned. "Watch out with those silly trucks."

"Go on! Go on!" muttered the trucks as

Percy pulled each one under the hopper.

"And by the way," Thomas went on,
"those buffers don't look very safe to
me . . ."

But he got no further. With a tremendous bump, the last truck passed the hopper much too fast. The coal poured down – all over Thomas.

"Help, I'm choking!" cried Thomas. "Get me out!"

Percy was worried, but he couldn't help laughing. Thomas's smart blue paint was covered in coal dust, from smoke-box to bunker.

"Ha! Ha!" chuckled Percy. "You don't look Really Useful now, Thomas. You look really disgraceful."

"I'm not disgraceful," choked Thomas. "You did that on purpose. Get me out!"

It took the men so long to clean Thomas
that he wasn't in time for his next train.

Toby had to take Annie and Clarabel
instead.

"Poor Thomas," whispered Annie and Clarabel. They were most upset.

Thomas was upset, too. He was very grumpy in the shed that night.

Toby thought it a great joke, but Percy was cross with Thomas for thinking that *he* had made Thomas's paint dirty on purpose.

"Fancy a Really Useful Blue engine like Thomas becoming a disgrace to the Fat Controller's railway!" said Percy. "Pooh! I wouldn't have missed all that fun for anything," he chuckled.

Thomas was at the platform the next day
when Percy brought his trucks in from the
junction. The trucks were heavy.

"I feel so tired," Percy puffed as he pulled
into the station.

"Have a drink," said his driver. "Then you'll feel better."

The water column stood at the end of the siding with the unsafe buffers. The props underneath the buffers were old and needed mending. Percy moved forward and found that he couldn't stop. The buffers didn't stop him either!

"Oooh," wailed Percy. "Help!"

The buffers were broken and Percy was
wheel-deep in coal.

It was time for Thomas to leave. He had seen everything.

"Now Percy has learnt his lesson, too," he chuckled to himself.

That night the two engines made up their quarrel.

"I didn't cause your accident on purpose, Thomas," whispered Percy. "You do know that, don't you?"

"Of course," replied Thomas. "And I'm sorry I was cheeky. Your green paint looks splendid again, too.

"In future, we'll both be more careful of coal," said Thomas wisely.

THOMAS

EDWARD

GORDON